THE THREE BILLY GOATS GRUFF

P. C. Asbjørnsen and J. E. Moe
Taken from the translation of G. W. Dasent

Pictures by
MARCIA BROWN

Voyager Books
Harcourt, Inc.
ORLANDO   AUSTIN   NEW YORK
SAN DIEGO   TORONTO   LONDON

To Anne Carroll Moore and the Troll

For information about permission to reproduce selections from this book,
please write Permissions, Houghton Mifflin Harcourt Publishing Company,
215 Park Avenue South, NY, NY 10003.

www.hmhbooks.com

Voyager Books *is a registered trademark of Harcourt, Inc.*

Library of Congress Cataloging-in-Publication Data
Asbjørnsen, Peter Christen, 1812–1885.
(Tre bukkene Bruse. English)
The three billy goats Gruff/P. C. Asbjørnsen and J. E. Moe; pictures by Marcia
Brown; (from the translation of G. W. Dasent).
p.   cm.
"Voyager Books."
Translation of: Tre bukkene Bruse.
Summary: The three billy goats outsmart the hungry troll who lives under the bridge.
ISBN-13: 978-0-15-690150-5 (pbk.)
ISBN-10: 0-15-690150-1 (pbk.)
(1. Fairy tales. 2. Folklore—Norway.)   I. Moe, Jørgen Engebretsen, 1813–1882.
II. Brown, Marcia, ill.   III. Title.
PZ8.A89Th   1991
398.24'5297358'09481–dc20   90-39587
(E)

Printed in China

LEO   20
4500468317

NCE on a time there were three billy goats who were to go up to the hillside to make themselves fat, and the name of all three was "Gruff."

On the way up was a bridge over a river they had to cross, and under the bridge lived a great ugly troll with eyes as big as saucers and a nose as long as a poker.

So first of all came the youngest
Billy Goat Gruff to cross the bridge.
"Trip, trap! trip, trap!" went the bridge.

"*Who's that tripping over my bridge?*" roared the troll.
"Oh, it is only I, the tiniest Billy
Goat Gruff, and I'm going up
to the hillside to make myself fat,"
said the billy goat with such a small voice.
"*Now, I'm coming to gobble you up!*" said the troll.

"Oh, no! pray don't take me. I'm too little, that I am," said the billy goat. "Wait a bit till the second Billy Goat Gruff comes. He's much bigger." "Well! be off with you," said the troll.

A little while after came the second
Billy Goat Gruff to cross the bridge.
"Trip, trap! trip, trap! trip, trap!"
went the bridge.

"*Who's that tripping over my bridge?*" roared the troll.
"Oh, it's the second Billy Goat Gruff,
and I'm going up to the hillside to
make myself fat," said the billy goat,
and his voice was not so small.

"*Now, I'm coming to gobble you up!*" said the troll.

"Oh, no! don't take me. Wait a little till the
big Billy Goat Gruff comes. He's much bigger."
"Very well! be off with you," said the troll.

Just then, up came the big Billy Goat Gruff.
"T-r-i-p, t-r-a-p! t-r-i-p, t-r-a-p!
t-r-i-p, t-r-a-p!" went the bridge, for the
billy goat was so heavy that the bridge
creaked and groaned under him.
"*Who's that tramping over my bridge?*" roared the troll.

"It's I! the
BIG BILLY GOAT
GRUFF!"
said the billy goat, who had an
ugly hoarse voice of his own.

"Now, I'm coming to gobble you up!" roared the troll.
 "Well, come along! I've got two spears,
 And I'll poke your eyeballs out at your ears.
 I've got besides two great big stones,
 And I'll crush you to bits, body and bones."

That was what the billy goat said; and so he flew at the troll, and poked his eyes out with his horns, and crushed him to bits, body and bones, and tossed him into the river.

Then he went up to the hillside.

There the billy goats got so fat they were
scarce able to walk again; and if the fat hasn't
fallen off them, why they're still fat; and so—
"Snip, snap, snout.
This tale's told out."